Dick Bruna

Boris
and Barbara

Big Tent Entertainment

New York

Boris has a little friend.

Her name is Barbara.

She has seven freckles.

Can you see where they are?

You can see them better here,

and Boris likes to say,

"My friend has seven freckles

and I like her just that way."

Then Boris said to Barbara,

"There's something you should see.

Let's take a walk and I'll show you

I can climb high up a tree."

So they walked to the forest

and into a very green spot.

Here the trees stood close together

and there were quite a lot.

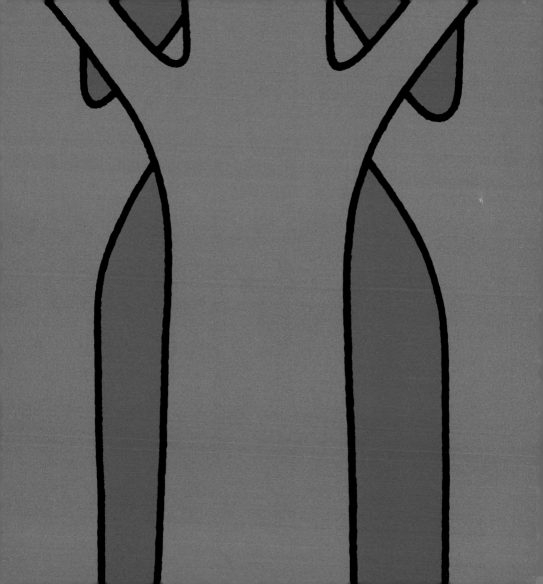

Then Boris said to Barbara,

"Just watch how quick I am."

He found a good strong tree trunk,

and he began to climb.

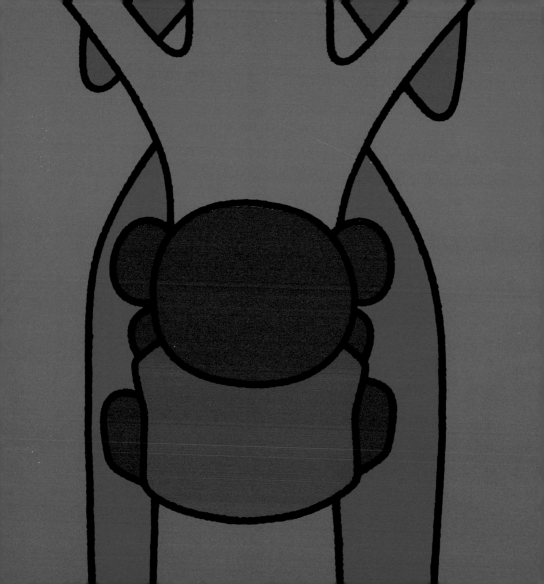

But Barbara was worried.

The tree was very tall.

"Be careful, Boris," Barbara cried.

"Be careful you don't fall!"

"Not me," said he. "It's easy.

Look, I'm not holding on.

Watch me walk along this branch..."

But then it all went wrong.

His foot slipped off, and Boris —

it was no fun at all —

landed much further down the tree.

It was a painful fall!

Then Boris, you can see his paws,

climbed slowly down again.

He was very careful now.

How silly he had been.

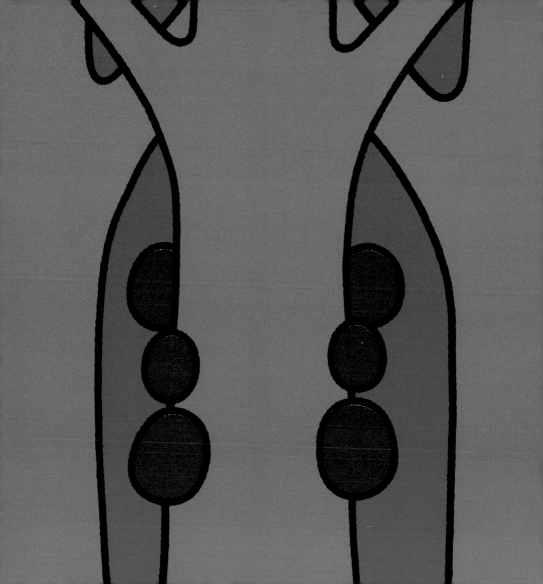

His cheek was really painful, too.

There seemed to be no relief.

Then Barbara said, "I'll run and get

a cold, wet handkerchief."

She ran out of the forest

and was quickly back again.

"Here, hold this hankie," Barbara said,

"just where you feel the pain."

The hankie was a good idea.

The pain was soon quite gone.

"The next time I climb," said Boris,

"I'll do it holding on!"

Big Tent Entertainment
111 East 14th Street, #127
New York, NY 10003

Originally published in 1989 as *boris en barbara* by Mercis Publishing bv, Amsterdam, Netherlands.
Original text Dick Bruna © copyright Mercis Publishing bv, 1989.
Illustrations Dick Bruna © copyright Mercis bv, 1989.

Published in the U.S. in 2003 by Big Tent Entertainment, New York.
Publication licensed by Mercis Publishing bv, Amsterdam, through Big Tent Entertainment.
English translation © copyright 2003 by Mercis Publishing bv.

ISBN: 1-59226-027-6
Library of Congress Control Number: 2002113026

Printed in Germany.

10 9 8 7 6 5 4 3 2 1